The Pen
Sam Hun

Sam Hunt was born in 1946 at Castor Bay, Auckland.
While his commitment to the writing of poetry came from
his mother and her side of the family, an equally strong
commitment, to poetry as performance, is also in his blood
— his father's side of the family were actors and troupers.
Hunt's own father was himself a man of the boards, a
somewhat eccentric barrister.

After being expelled from school Hunt hitch-hiked
south, where Alistair Campbell gave the young poet the
direction he needed. There followed the many and often
spectacular forays into a variety of jobs — truck driving,
schoolteaching, panel-beating — and in 1975 a stint as
the Robert Burns Fellow at Otago University. But his
vocation was, and remains to be, the writing and
performing of his poems and songs.

Over the years Sam Hunt has made his home around
various parts of the Pauatahanui estuary — Bottle Creek
where sheep-dog Minstrel joined the Hunt entourage,
Battle Hill where son Tom was born to Sam and Kristin in
1976, Deaths Corner, and more recently Red Rocks on
Cook Strait — places that have provided the necessary
peace and space when not on the road around New Zealand
and Australia.

Sam Hunt
Collected Poems 1963–1980

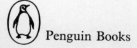

Penguin Books

Penguin Books Ltd, Harmondsworth,
Middlesex, England
Penguin Books, 625 Madison Avenue,
New York, New York 10022, U.S.A.
Penguin Books Australia Ltd, Ringwood,
Victoria, Australia
Penguin Books Canada Ltd, 2801 John Street,
Markham, Ontario, Canada L3R IB4
Penguin Books (N.Z.) Ltd, 182-190 Wairau Road,
Auckland 10, New Zealand

First published 1980
Reprinted 1981, 1983
Copyright © Sam Hunt 1980
All rights reserved

Printed in Hong Kong by
Wah Cheong Printing Press Ltd.

Contents

Acknowledgements

The publishers would like to acknowledge the following in which some of the poems in this collection first appeared: *Ako Pai, Argot, Arts Festival Yearbook 1968, Arts and Community, Cave, Climate, Comment, Dominion, Dunedin Star, 4 New Zealand Poets* (New Zealand Students' Arts Council, 1979), *Islands, Landfall, New Poetry,* NZBC Poetry Programme, *NZ Herald, NZ Listener, New Zealand Poetry, Nova, Otago Review, Poems for the Eighties* (Wai-te-ata Press, 1979), *Poetry Australia, Poet India, Poetry New Zealand* (Vols 1, 2, 3 and 4), *Salient,* Television New Zealand, 'Wonder World' (Channel 10, Sydney), and 'Writing' (Radio New Zealand).

Some poems were first published in the *School Journal* (Department of Education), some were first published in broadsheet form by the Triple P Press, and 'Postcard of a Cabbage Tree' was first published as a broadsheet by the Bottle Press.

Seven collections of Sam Hunt's poetry have been published, in which many of the poems in this book first appeared: *Between Islands,* Sam Hunt, 1963; *From Bottle Creek Selected Poems 1965-69,* Arts Council/Teachers College, 1969; *Bracken Country,* Glenbervie Press, 1971; *From Bottle Creek,* Alister Taylor Publishing Ltd, 1972; *South Into Winter,* Alister Taylor Publishing Ltd, 1973; *Time To Ride,* Alister Taylor Publishing Ltd, 1975; and *Drunkard's Garden,* Hampson Hunt, 1978.

Ngawhatu

(to Biddy on her fiftieth birthday)

1 Daybreak at the Hospital

In the asylum, as on a shore
Between far hills and sea, the people pace
The white-washed dial of their sunless years
Waiting the closed sky's flowering; and trace
Their courses towards the day's Madonna pity
Of blue silences.

The sun in the east like a steel flower
Yawns, and then from hills reaches to the sky;
Night falls down some far-off sea. The inmates
Stumble blind down concrete paths to wild
Light and siren cries. On insane whiteness,
The asylum in day rises.

2 Lady of the Tides

From sea along the sun's arc blue
herons lope through sky over wards
and the pacing inmates; then borne
from heights to a western shore like dew
to wind-ripped seas, the herons with wings
spread-out on a red sun sink.

Hysterical, the out-run ocean drives
into the wide shore's prostrate limbs
clawed waves, sharpened by slicing winds.
And now, as from dusk towards night
the waters frothing slowly climb
the torn altar of the crucified,

1

an inmate, Lady of the Tides,
stumbles from her white-washed room
through stations of the climbing moon;
and Lady waxing in her rise
over the slipping estuary,
drowns cries beneath in pendulous peace

like herons on the Ngawhatu
white siren sky of day; and in
her rising enfolds the beaten
altar in deep Madonna blue.

Letter Home

When things get too hard to bear
row out and catch the tide,
our blue dinghy stacked with beer;
ride the drift whichever way
as long as that long tide and half
the cold brown bottles last;
don't fear you'll ever be lost.

And if by the end of today
you catch the turned tide, love,
you'll be home back in our bay,
the two black cats catching sprats,
gulls scavenging for the catch,
at the end of the first day
since they sent me away.

Snowman in the Sun

This night my sleep has peopled
men, vague on far high slopes of
darkness. All night they've wandered
by, small and as if lost, scared
in the night through which they move.
But passing, they have distilled

themselves, a colourless band
of cloudy men, sad figures
all, upon my sleep: until
now in such light, I can't tell
them from this, the dawn they fuse;
— into which they merge, outlined

now: one man. My tall white man
of snow, alone as the day
he reigns. My Daddy! you, our
Snowman in the Sun! who towers
the great mountain we kids played
upon, sang and beat you down,

will now forever reign: in
each small kiss of snow before
the dawn, until the silent
hour, watching our mountain melt.
— And so melting, hour by hour
into the night, once again

my sad company of sleep
parade. I wake: in darkness
a small boy climbs; a tall man,
white, down a whitening mountain,
bows. And the boy sets on this
man's bowed head a bright red cap.

Letter to Mike Richards

The Riverhead Garden Bar,
any afternoon you choose:
no fears so long as we are
able to keep on the booze.

I'm okay, but find it so
bloody hard down here to find
a cobber who's in the know
and still say, yes let's get blind.

Hawks right now being hard to tame,
I usually drink alone —
small wonder my verse keeps time,
seven syllables a line!

What I'm really saying is,
I'll be up a week from this.
Give Fats a foot up the arse,
the Merc a full tank of gas.

Flutemaker
(a lament)

More regular than clockwork,
the sad retired captain down
the dune path would hobble for
sands where all night oceans break,
and with the sunlight roam,
dazed, the orphanage of the shore.

Poised like day he would then scan
forms abandoned by surf the
night before . . . gnomons now on
a sun-struck dial of shore;
and like the day, move through the
arc traced out by the flotsam.

Many white years later, late
one evening, the bent captain
found the form he'd searched so long
from which he would carve a flute;
marry his dry silences,
age and frailty, in song.

Up in his shack on the dunes
he chiselled all through the night,
until when day broke he knew
his brittle labour was done:
so the captain pursing tight
dry lips, down the white shaft blew.

And dark, giving itself up
in long slivers to distilled

shrill white shafts of morning sun,
left sunlight dancing on the
bent shadow of a crippled
captain whistling on the dunes.

My White Ship

Although together we
Drift the bay's slow pull
Of tides and know this sea
Behind the island will
Never drag us away,
And drifting lift not one
White sail to trap the day
Nor catch the sun,

The ethic of my love
For you remains that I
Am a lone sailer of
The night; captain of my
White ship: and though you be
A good day's mate, your fight's
Too weak to ride with me
These wild black nights.

So lie please in the peace of
Your anchored sleep, and do
Not cry for help, my love,
As if I'm drowning you,
But lie on without fright
When I raise my sail up
And ride out on the night
On my white ship.

Invocation in Equinox

Ozone floats for days, sweet and
heavy on the heaving wind:

all along the beach, washed-up
logs will lie like us asleep.

This is how it always is
this time of year, always,

every March, the equinox
brings storm: as now: black winds knock

at the rusty French doors till
you're sure Death has come to call. . . .

But forget your fears. I, too,
cannot sleep tonight although

I've been through many storms. Do
not worry, please. . . . Tomorrow

morning I'll take you for a
short walk round our yawn of bay

and let you, child, roam the shore —
you'll find there's nothing to fear;

then lead you slowly home, up
past the heaving logs to sleep.

Homecoming

1 'Rainy Day Woman'

The woman you made me is
copper, coal, beads and painted glass,
hung high, a world of colour
in my universe of rain.

She is, while you're away,
my woman for a rainy day.

Each morning I plait her wire
the golden copper of her hair,
then hang her from the rafters
so she knows the day is hers.

She watches like a cynic
as I knock the whiskies back —
until the final drink is done
when I curse that I was born,
and blame my drunken stupor on
the sadness in the falling rain . . .

and I watch my coal-and-beaded
copper-haired and painted bride

let her cynic's look fall down
and turn her colours in the rain.

2 The Bay

Last night the world was as black
as the black shag on the rock,

but now the morning has come
and tomorrow you come home;

my 'Rainy Day Woman' waits....

Yes, this morning with a new
sun spinning white on the blue

even the giant shag sits,
black wings tilted like kites:

and as heat from sunlight throbs
through the stirring bay, salt globes

of water bristle like sweat
on its outstretched wings. We wait.

The black shag splinters the light.

Singing For You Now

I'd rambled on, uncertain of
My songs, vague memories of love,
   Sung them two years now,
When really knowing nothing more
Than empty bottles round the floor;
   Waking, doomed, at noon.

But then two months ago you came
Bringing me your childlike calm,
   Something wholly new —
To wake up with the first light breaking
Through your dark, lashed eyes; and making
   Love, not song, to you.

   And now I gather you
Dry firewood and flowers from the cliff,
And lastly this, this song plucked live
   From silence, love,

   Singing for you now.

Christina 1

I need no woman's flesh to
climb and hide myself inside
tonight.... Right now, instead,
I load the grate with a few

fat logs from the beach. All these
months alone on whisky and
now the firewood on the sand,
the lovers laid like dinghies

anchored for the night; I load
myself with drink. There's a storm
blowing up tonight. Not that I'm
scared. But something must explode.

Plea Before Storm

Like the sky-high seagulls
tossed from those thundering black
boulders of the clouds, you are
girl, setting off back home,
looking for the things you've lost —
a mislaid purse and raincoat,
wondering where you put them last;
and nearly ready now to climb
the cliffpath, trying to recall
the home you left for this,
what way you came.

The macrocarpa blackness
quickens; pine-belts black on the hills.

Storm is coming in that crazed
rustle of leaves, the frenzied
laughter of the seagulls skidding
spread-eagled on the light. Like ice
setting, the light sets hard.

It is coming fast. Lightning
and thunder quicken. No pause.

I'm sorry, forget what I said.
Come back inside.

Young Girl Watching Mist

Gabriel, the coast hills heave through mist.
They'd have no place but for the radio mast
Shafted in storm light. Don't worry, they'll be there,
The hills, long after you have gone from here.

In that mist up there there is no up and down.
Run fast and you find you're pedalling air
To nowhere on your head. So stay in the garden.
Up in that mist you could be anywhere.

Yes stay right there. For all you know, that mast
Could be just a shaft of light. And maybe the mist
Has rolled the hills away. And I will watch from here
Young girl, you look so good. You stay there.

The Gulls

At night the gulls fly back to
rock ledges.

       A volcanic
island, I remember. Grey
sea, the grey sky quickening to
blackness. And the gulls, black-backed
but white, white underwing, they
return in legions to rock
ledges of the night. And this
place, too, I know. A bunk-like
ledge where I crouch on black
stones with a woman, and kiss
her till she quickens. The link
with her, black to black.

               While high
overhead, we watch white legions
of gulls circling . . . until giddy,
we spin into sleep.

         And I
find next morning, pecked remains
of some woman beside me.

                   Rangitoto Island

At Castor Bay

I found the colour of your
flesh again this morning:
a tidal bank exposed
at dead low water, shells
the colour of your flesh.

This coast again . . . sun rising
over islands this blue May
morning reefed inside the bay
where sunlight floods:
wading to my knees, fat
black seagulls on the smooth hard sand
and water clapping, the rock-pools
drained . . . familiar
but no less bright,
your silken crevices.

A White Gentian

Remember Ruapehu,
that mountain, six months ago?
You sat in an alpine hut
sketching scoria, red
rusted outcrops in the snow.

I climbed some southern peak
and made up the sort of song
men climbing mountains sing:
how, no longer your lover,
I knew it was over.

I thought I'd try out my song
when I returned that evening
as though there were nothing wrong.
Instead I brought a flower down
smelling of the mountain.

A Purple Balloon

1
As father to five children
they say he failed. Drinking
whisky for a week non-stop,
at every gulp, blinking,
at the wonder of it all,
the same blue eyes my mother
sometimes says she sees in me.
My grandfather was, they say,
a failure of the first degree.

And every Christmas Day, our
drunk old Santa Claus, he came,
with a pohutukawa
flower stuck like a clotted bloom
of blood on his coat lapel:
pockets full: always his green
bottle with its latch-on cap;
singing with us kids till all
we could do was yell and clap. . . .

The last Christmas he came he
gave me a purple balloon.

When turned twelve I hitch-hiked
north to Waiotu: run-down
farms and eroded hills; clay,
skylines gaping red with clay;
spending Easter with him in
his shack of fibrolite and tin:

for the three days drinking wine
he'd crushed from grape and let
ferment in an old tin can.....

Hangover sun and Sunday,
songs and a purple balloon.

2
When gangrene set in, my
grandfather's feet on a rack,
laid in a hospital bed
he watched them slowly turn black.
But even after they'd cut
both his legs to the knee, still
he claimed he could twitch his toes
and would ask for flowers at night
and what they'd done with his shoes.

Waiting the priest, no one
seemed to know quite what to do.
My mum watched the empty pit.
Hands behind their backs, the grave-
diggers wore white denim coats.
And after the priest had come
and gone, and the white men slid
the coffin down, we all dropped
paper poppies on the lid.....

I tried to believe but couldn't
forget the purple balloon.

Drinking all day in this far
north harbour pub, I couldn't

help think of him, now dead. (With
salt and whisky on his breath,
some sand-barred sailor locals
here still talk about, who stalks
the sand-bar singing where he
drowned one night: drunk, rolling
drunk on whisky down the bar....)

I couldn't help but think of his
night; and a purple balloon.

Sunday Evening

This morning gathering wood
at the old mill up Moonshine
Valley Road: all a little
pointless, these fires, with no one
here but myself a little
drunk and out of booze.

                  And all
the afternoon, combed the edge
of the estuary, kindling
for a month.

          With an almost
sickening smell of gum, night
settles in the macrocarpas.

The first sharp drops of cold rain
fall. I think of her, five foot,
no more, maybe dead: a black
raven crouching in her thighs.

A Song About Her

My liquor bill cut by half
up from two years with the dead
I've ripped my faded pin-ups down
kicked my pillows out of bed.

Trotting her home last night
down past Mount Street Cemetery
my silent girl she said how much
she hoped she'd soon see more of me.

Then as yesterday at Makara Beach
I did not try the ancient move
for fear I would destroy
what only time and silence do.

Two years out of practice
writing cool Platonic songs about
a girl too innocent to seize
the hot rod of a V8 lout,

I'm singing now because the shellbanks
shine and in the sun here, sober,
smoking her last night's butts,
I know I love her.

East Coast Bay

Along hard sand a daughter
leads her old mother beside
the early morning water.
Ma's a crumpled nanny goat.

Looking at her now, it's clear
plum will be today's colour
(incredible to think,
every pleat and wrinkle of
this walking mummy — plum pink!)

And she is sitting down now
on one of the brand new
Council benches erected
especially for old people.

Feet crossed on the rests provided,
her plum pink slippers hang like
slices from her stockinged toes.
She squints out at the bright sea
astonished to be awake.

The Wait
(for Janet)

For these last couple of months
autumn has dripped from the branches.
But daylight now, a gibbous moon,
the first morning of the winter term.
And already we wait winter rains.

Late on at some party one wet
Saturday night we watched rain set
spinnakers across the city.
But it must've been just drizzle for
we watched outside an hour or more.

And these months since then when we met
I've tried writing you a verse letter.
But the more I tried for word and rhyme
the less I could forget my father.
Everything I wrote is about him.

But it's June now, full of winter
images that may anger old lovers,
my first of you; the branches set hard:
a heron as cold as the blue
morning crouched on the shallows;

this sky of the city where you live
rigid with cranes. And two pale rainbows.
We've waited . . . and still must wait,
watching cold sunlight lean, white
winter sails on the shadows.

Wish for an Air-Trip North

After three weeks together in the shack,
How could you ever have expected me
To play our parting cool . . . simply
Kiss you, wave goodbye and turn my back?

Your first time up. I waved like a windsock
As your plane took off. Then no one to see,
Brought a bottle of hard stuff home. Now empty
And me very drunk. Hope you don't feel as sick.

Deep in a plush red seat with safety belt slack,
You probably took it all as easily,
The take-off thrust, as you did taking me.

So all my last wish is, that the joy-stick
Bring you, darling, down so carefully
It brings to mind our night trips in the sack.

Photograph of Robin

Over-exposed, the background bushes bear
white light like snow where leaves should be.
You'd be running towards them, away down flights
of steps; but have stopped in fright.

The light is intense down there
but cold. And like a bewildered moth
you've paused. . . . You are pulling your hair
more tightly round your mouth.

Photograph of Robin in War-Paint

Those big eyes they are like black
stones emerging through the snow.
Spring has made the mountains cry,
the whites of your wide eyes thaw.. . .

Come on, no tears now!

I have seen you often, mouth
puckered and your hair undone.
Even war-paint on your face
won't frighten me, dear Indian:

I have so often watched you
painting it all on, and know
the cheeky girl who tries to
startle adults with a show.

But they are not interested.
They've already decided
long-haired cowboys should be scalped
and pretty Indians shot dead.. . .

Come on, off to bed.

Max

There are no mountains in the
part of the country Max lived.
And he'd nothing on his walls
except a window that looked
nowhere in particular;
a give-away calendar
from the store on the corner,
(six colour shots, each one was
meant to last two months).

Over the five years we were
each other's best friend, Max's
calendar stayed open on
May-June 1954,
one of Queenstown and mountains.
It wasn't for the picture
of the town and lake, I'm sure,
Max left it open there;
but for the mountains rather.

His three older brothers all
had photographs of football
teams and score-sheets on their walls.
But they were older, and soon
left home for distant jobs, left Max
alone for years. . . . Later on
when Max left, he packed crampons,
a pick and his calendar.
He was ready for the mountains.

Gauguin Through Fever
(for Prue and Jerry Ursell)

1
The mud shines, pock-marked after rain.
The tide is on an inward run
Cockle-shells floating on its back:
A day for sleeping in the sun. . . .

But such an occupation
Demands you lie so still
You may well be taken
And buried for dead

No matter how you scream.

2
I have, instead, gazed at Gauguin's
Painting, birth in a barn.
The girl on a bright yellow bed
Her colourless cat at her feet. . . .

Dullness of black-out tangles
Two cattle in the corner:
Her child has just been born
And she lies as in fever

Too tired to scream.

3
Another fever mine,
But I love that sleeping cat,
Its each eye live as a star.
Rats of delirium are white. . . .

No safe South Sea Island dream,
This painting in your room:
I have watched it through a fever
Shake until the cattle stir

And colours scream.

July 21 1969

I read you an angry man's
    poem of war-time in Milan,
1944.... Two years
    you say, before we were born
and this went on, it's crazy!
        (A pop star died last month. Two men
this morning walked on the moon.)

Nothing shocks anyone now...
    when I read of Jones's death
it should have been as impersonal
    as that bathroom in the station.
But it stunned me somehow —
    as if, with a tap on the door,
I'd been joined by the queer custodian.

I know many our age have died
    but when by suicide
it's something more than death.
    The bathroom roared like an oven.
I coughed steam. Clenched my eyes to it.
    But nothing shocks anyone, even
men on the moon. I like the old poems.

Ice on the Jetty
(*Rebecca*, 5)

My mother died and there's no
school. And later in the week
I am going with my father
south to where he works.

We're going to live where there are
lots of cats, some stray,
that feed from tight-mouthed herring jars
and sit on the jetty all day.

I've been there sometime before . . .
it's like an enormous room
my mother would talk about
that people sat in in her dreams.

She said she never knew
who any of them were.
Their faces would spread into walls
and then they'd all smile at her.

She used to wake me screaming
then make a pot of tea. . . .
I know I've been there.
There was ice on the jetty.

Somewhere Near Here, Many Miles

Somewhere near here, many miles,
this night of rain is falling
hard on corrugated iron
inlet shacks. Here, soft on tiles;

and if the door weren't open
it may just as well be yet
another comfortable night,
the electric blanket on . . .

the rain hitting down hard while
this State suburb sleeps: you would
hardly know . . . another world
somewhere near here; many miles.

Porirua

Porirua Friday Night

Acne blossoms scarlet on their cheeks,
These kids up Porirua East.... .
Pinned across this young girl's breast
A name-tag on the supermarket badge;
A city-sky-blue smock.
Her face unclenches like a fist.

Fourteen when I met her first
A year ago, she's now left school,
Going with the boy
She hopes will marry her next year.
I asked if she found it hard
Working in the store these Friday nights
When friends are on the town.

She never heard:
But went on, rather, talking of
The house her man had put
A first deposit on
And what it's like to be in love.

A Summer Poem

We would never build our huts
in macrocarpa trees:
the brooding darkness, wetness,
in darker greenness was
where wetas and those birds
that peck your eyes out lived.

Sun and the smell of the gum,
we built instead in the pines,
hoisting with ropes limb to limb
planks from the timber yard;
and other days we would use
the ropes as swings. . . .

A friend once swung to a roar
some forty feet up —
the highest that summer —
the rope tied to nothing more
than a peg of a limb.
The whole next week he was King.

Black Toadstools

Black toadstools grow best under
pines, among red needles where
their only moisture is the
dripping branches.
                    Black toadstools:
others I recall, orange
as they were poisonous, huge
white blotches on their backs.
                              We
children had a tree hut in
a pine. I lay there often
looking down, watching all the
sparrows, a magpie sometimes,
pecking at the ground.
                    But those
birds knew exactly what was
what they should eat. They never
used them, even when it rained.
Like us they had houses and
just liked looking down.
                    But one
quick afternoon, after rain,
raindrops dripping still, the sun
broke through. I think I must have
been asleep. I looked down and saw
those toadstools big as black
umbrellas. With a fall I
woke up shivering, my back
wet; face down. The toadstools were
poisonous; black umbrellas with
polka-dots white as sun-drops.

When Morning Comes
(a flat fat blues)

Grab you for
a yawning kiss
feel your tongue
when morning comes
it only is
the old mattress

a-climbing babe
climbing to your flat
when morning comes
I greet you babe
greet you with a big
good morning fat

there beside you
little girl
lost in wheat
fields of light
when morning comes
inside you Sweet

my honey baby
let me be
your little boy
a whole night long
a-let me be
your Daddy too

when morning comes
into my room
without a knock

and goes again
without a bang
I'm left alone

I'm left a drunk
old baritone
singing like a
flat saxophone
when morning comes
without you Sweet.

A Bottle Creek Blues

The wind can't blow any harder,
the air's as heavy as Hell . . . .

I watched blue diesel smoke like mist
hanging on a high suburban hill:
wind I thought would blow it away
but the wind itself is diesel.

And yet the smoke disappeared
absorbed by that suburban hill:
the problem of disposal was
solved by the lungs of the people.

Two years ago we used to row
to an island here called Cockleshell:
gather cockles in a sack,
warm them up and gorge ourselves.

A friend I used to do this with
near died from typhoid fever:
they had the cockles analysed —
shit from down the coastline further.

Barefeet on the beach is madness,
this beach that was once made of sand:
the sun shines bright on broken glass,
cockles from Cockleshell Island are banned.

Sad protest songs are sung and heard
like this one here. And afterwards
the audience goes home convinced
the shit's cleared clean away with words. . . .

The wind can't blow any harder,
the air's too heavy for the birds.

A Hot-Water Bottle Baby Blues

All that I love alive I've killed,
nothing to save, still less to lose:
these nights I suffer from the cold
hot-water bottle baby blues.

An afternoon I left you tucked
trembling like a rain-downed bird
beneath a bank, and three times tacked
my way upstream, but soon was bored.

I raced a log back down the stream
until, still underneath the bank,
I found you crouched. It was no dream.
You asked me for a piggyback.

Clutching lightly as a bird,
warm heart beating on my back, you grinned,
waving your arms round as I bowed —
and just like that we left the ground.

We flew all night until I could
fly no more . . . and falling, felt you lose
your warmth. . . . I woke up with the cold
hot-water bottle baby blues.

A Sandshoe Shuffle

I don't know where I walked
how many faces I kicked
   all I know now
   I'm sorry babe
sorry I somehow missed

The boy, out there, he says
   he's sorry too
I think he should soon be through
   so honey when you
   can give me your time
·   I'll give you a rhyme
I'll say I'm sorry too

I've done some groping around this room
two men they're groping round the moon
   they're after peace
   yeah a 2-cent piece
they'll both give you a call in time

But your sandpaper boy
   he won't say goodbye
I guess he feels he can't get through
   so honey if you
   could loan me a dime
   I'll call you sometime
I want to say I'm sorry too

I'll make it sometime round midnight
make sure you're somewhere about
   'cause if you're not
   well woman watch out
I'll do the sandshoe shuffle for you

My Father Scything

My father was sixty when I was born,
twice my mother's age. But he's never been
around very much, neither at the mast
round the world; nor when I wanted him most.
He was somewhere else, like in his upstairs
Dickens-like law office counting the stars;
or sometimes out with his scythe on Sunday
working the path through the lupins toward the sea.

And the photograph album I bought myself
on leaving home, lies open on the shelf
at the one photograph I have of him,
my father scything. In the same album
beside him, one of my mother.
I stuck them there on the page together.

Return in Spring

1

At war all day in the buffalo grass,
Our backs would itch all night. And each tall pine,
Five of them, stirred as if by sea-winds in the mind;
Raw smell of gum where we'd hammered nails in.

Tree-huts in their limbs: mine, the last one down
The section from the house. Once a summer bach
This place, sprawled over the years, room on room,
like lupin down the run-down garden to the beach.

2

I have no memories as others do
Of family outings: we had it all here,
White sand, ocean, Wairau Creek and bridge,
The orchard where we laid our bodies bare.

The lupin too, a lattice-work of dens
Deep in foliage . . . down a corridor
Of green October light, a small boy knocked
His first girl up, shoving through her bolted door.

3

I took all this this morning, piece by piece,
And nothing seemed the same. The corridors
Through the lupins and down the pine tree limbs
Were splayed; and where were huts and dens, claws.

Only later, when I had been along the beach
And seen again the orchard, bridge and creek,
Could I recall each hut, and find that still
The pine trees bleed where once our nails struck.

Before the Demolitions
(for Janet)

A groper boat has just tied up, fresh
from days in the Straits. They unload their fish.
And a woman in a small bikini
catches herrings in a jar.... Here the sea
joins hands, the tides do whirlpools;
tin shacks squat on piles
between State Highway One and
the railway bridge ... you came in the end

in love or out of love. But a barge
is tethered today by the bridge,
a railway gang with chainsaws there.
They lay new jarra sleepers. And some other
day soon, some gang will bulldoze us out.
Until then we learn to love by heart.

Slug Alley

Letter to Jerusalem 1

1
Over the years I've pinned
faith on many women,
given them all I owned
to be their kind of man

and now do little more
than please their each sweet whim:
I'm pushing twenty-four
in need of guidance, Jim:

because all I know —
all cuff and rotten breath
black-eyed and bloodshot now —
is that I need a bath

in an Akitio spring,
clamber wet the autumn
riverbanks, a pilgrim
towards Jerusalem.

2
Impossible in talk
or verses to resolve
these riddles that will take
me to the grave to solve.

I've asked your contemporaries
the answers and the facts
but find their hang-up is
the over-forty fuck.

Odd enough, I found more out
in a Sunday newspaper
double-page splurge about
a man who found a pauper

propped inside himself, a stubble-
faced and faceless man;
how in his steps he stumbled
towards Jerusalem.

3
But you see I'm far
from any answers yet.
But that's what I'm after
with the toe-jam and sweat.

With these wiped away
it's all too easy
to think that all's OK:
a game of Happy Family,

a plate-glass harbour view,
regular teaching job
and regular screw,
the occasional jab;

holidays hire a jet-boat
return to Oblivion.... .
I think the wiser bet
is one-way to Jerusalem.

Letter to Jerusalem 2

On the skyline of the Kaiwhara hills,
Gill, a mother to the kids on pills
Keeps open house, sends you her love.
Johnny too, who may forget to leave
For work some mornings in the woolstore
Sits drinking in the sun outside the door:
Tall buildings no bigger than blocks on the floor,
Wellington afloat on the harbour haze. . . .
You think of how most men spend their days
In offices as cramped as elevators —
Their wish, to be heading Heavenwards,
'Up in the world' to use their words!
The law they all ignore, of gravity,
My friends at Kaiwhara and I
Observe in this old house against the sky . . .
The Fall. Whatever. The sun on the sea.
Too much of this good life, I'll go dry!

Summer coming, Sylvia and I will sleep
Together often in the sun — and slip
A long way off, a long way from the beat
And hurt of words. And wake, carnal with heat.

I got round to thinking I'd better reply,
I owe you a letter, Old Father Sky,
Tell you what I'm up to. I hitch-hiked out
This afternoon to Bottle Creek,
Could easily have made it with the chick
Who picked me up: I've little doubt
She'd very much fancy a denim lout —
A little rougher than her easy-action

Husband who fails to bring her on.
She went out of her way, drove me right home.
I didn't try. Instead, told her this poem
I'm now writing down.

                Did I want to travel?
She asked, and nearly slid on the gravel
When I told her my only ambition
Was to make a perfect act of contrition,
And when I grew up, to be a moonshiner
Whisky-mad and bare-back on the hills,
And to fart as loud as an ocean-liner.

But the world, old cock, is hard on my heels.
The truth is, Jim, the Education Board
Is gunning me down with a 3-year bond
To teach young kids a cursive script
Tidy as a row of angels' holes,
To teach the kids that if they have to shit
To clean up afterwards and keep clean souls.

It's hard, but there we are! I think by now
You'll have the message strong. I don't know how,
But very soon I'm off outside to join
Johnny for a beer . . . and toss a coin
Late on some summer afternoon.
Whichever way it falls, I'll see you soon.

You Comfort Him

Kids from upper-income suburbs come
In nylon parkas, raw wool caps, this
Cold Sunday afternoon, the year's
Shortest day.... Sandshoes on the white
Sharp path of shell. Fishermen and their wives or
Lovers live in rainbow-coloured
Shacks on stilts around this shore.

They are dancing on our jetty, these
Children of the golf-club. Not long
Before night falls; and the dew: before
One slips on the breakneck ramp.
Yet again he'll turn, see you, let
You comfort him. He will not remember
Tomorrow. Today he turns. It is Sunday, Mary.

8 p.m. 'World of Science'

The man on the radio
explains the way the winds blow.
I sigh.
      I just don't follow.
      This child here's
no better. Yet his kites fly.

He Is Who Is; Your Love
(for Jenny and Ray Lilley)

This is the season we turn
offers of employment down.
So to this merry-go-round
band rotunda of a bar;
we drink local Hawke's Bay beer,
talk of some other harbour.

Here again to walk this earth-
quake beach where black-faced orange
marigolds push through flint,
a gannet cape divides blue
sea, blue sky . . . in love or out
of love, adopted by you

friends, travellers too, I come
offer you my hand, accept
your tourniquet to grief, your
love my wrist. I know nothing
better: the son you adopt,
a name-tag bound to his wrist,

he is the love you accept.

Smash
(for Meg)

Moths on the farmhouse window
batter like rain on the glass:
they're allowed a half-inch gap
where I left the door ajar.

I have sat here hours watching.
And now at last one's made it,
a dizzy lady off course.
She flutters on white-hot light.

And still on the window-pane
a million more moths outside....
Watch them skid! how they collide
and trickle down with the rain.

Postcard of a Cabbage Tree

1

Pith where hard heart should be.
Climb but never hope to find
Anything but blossoms for a mind.
I'm more a lily than a tree.

And ignore the picture please.
I'm not what it makes out I am.
Just rip it up and call me Sam,
An old flat-footed cabbage tree.

2

Few believe in what they see.
Your friends prefer to call it myth
Passed down by drunken word of mouth:
They say such things just cannot be,

That in the spring a heavy
Blossom forecasts summer drought.
Forget them please, don't ever doubt
An old flat-footed cabbage tree.

3

And don't come here to study.
These brackish winds up Bottle Creek
Would make the best mind crack.
It's safer in some library.

Come rather for the early
Mornings waking in the bach,
At the south end of the beach
An old flat-footed cabbage tree.

4
And please don't probe the heart in me
Initialling your own
Name deep into my bone.
You'll end up on your knees

Wondering how you let this be-
Come the tombstone of our love,
Knelt at the knotted ankles of
An old flat-footed cabbage tree.

5
And so to ramble on all night.
So easy, finding images
Of proper postcard size.
But none of them are right.

I'm nothing more than what you see . . .
At my feet, Pied Piper boots
Standing, where I must collapse,
An old flat-footed cabbage tree.

Her Words on Leaving

I began to wake in suburbs
padding cold concrete for
a 4-bottle plastic crate.
The last house in the street.

Wrought iron hedges the garden.
It keeps the hill from rolling
flat and away, our unborn
children in. . . .

The man at the hospital
said Drink lots of milk.
I woke up a long time later,
a cap of curlers for hair.

But I soon have to leave. . . .
People always told me
Travel while you can, you're young.
I've travelled all my life.

I'm not sick. But I hate,
fear more than your coming, the grate
of tubular steel on iron,
the click of the gate.

A School Report

Working with these young kids in the pastel
clay frontier, we live near bulldozer blades.
The school I came to yesterday had loads
of children waiting: that was all.
The road up the valley still a shingle path.
The town planners never predicted such birth.

They write short poems, the kids. 'I wish I was rich I
wish I had gold wings I am made out of sky . . . .'
They paint houses pastel, and the houses
smudge. I told them this morning how wild horses
and moonshiners lived here once. Late on today
a group of them made a model city of clay.

Saturday Palm Sunday

I live on a long inlet
often write down lines about it
songs that people living in
the suburbs and the cities sing.

This morning when I rowed across
the channel to the bottle store
two pied oystercatchers were
padding on a mudbank.

This afternoon with a shy friend,
cold beer on the jetty,
talk about the week just over
and how the oystercatcher feeds;

drive up Moonshine later on,
drink more, a harsh home wine,
cook sausages and know you're gone,
no reason now to write songs down.

A Valley Called Moonshine
(*for Josh Andersen*)

The lights in the farmhouses
go out. The inlet is out.

An iron shack on the shoreline
floats its light on the water.

A grandfather up Moonshine
remembers the first daughter.

Dreams are easy. Wild horses.

A Mangaweka Roadsong

No place more I'd like to bring you than
this one-pub town
approached in low gear down
the gorges through the hills.

Now they've built the by-pass
the drinkers left are locals
& odd commercial travellers.
Quiet afternoons like this you hear the falls.

On the Post Office corner
a blue flag floats. I bought
a hot meat pie at the store,
a new harmonica.

A public bar drinker
tells me what I want to hear.
I play for him later
songs on my harmonica.

We know each other now.
I buy my round of beers,
I catch up on the news
in small town public bars.

They ask me why I travel
& never settle down.
I lose two games of pool
& hitch-hike out of town.

Beware the Man

Beware the man who tries to fit you out
In his idea of a hat
Dictating the colour and the shape of it.

He takes your head and carefully measures it
Says 'Of course black's out.'
He sees himself in the big black hat.

So you may be a member of the act
He makes for you your special coloured hat.
Beware! He's fitting you for more than that.

School Policy on Stickmen

It's said that children should not use
stick figures when they draw!
And yet I've lain all night awake
looking at this drawing here
of orange men, stick figures every one of them,
walking up a crayon mountain hand in hand
walking up my wall.

They're edging up a ridge
their backs against the mountain
pinned against my wall.
And every one is smiling.
They know the way a mountain laughs,
especially crayon mountains made of brown.
They know they're not allowed,
these orange men.

Walking the Morning City

Walking the morning city
the opposite direction
workers walking toward me
walking from the sun:
I have no job to go to
so walk into the station

watch the all-night Limited
pull in at the platform
pretend I'm waiting for
a friend who never came:
pretend I'm disappointed
vamp my blues harmonica

buy a lightweight pad
& biro at the station store
coffee at the cafeteria
pretend to write a letter:
have no one to write to
so drink a cup & leave

walk down morning streets
lightweight in the sun
no one to tell this to
'cause no one is my lover.
This morning more than ever
I'm set on finding you.

Post Office Report

'No space for human error,'
the postmaster tells me,
'they're a team my workers here.'

Morning tea-break I meet the team:
efficient, incredibly
ugly every one of them.

Understaffed? in need maybe
of extra office space? I suggest
an arm-chair for pension day.

My report goes on, every
date-stamp initialled and timed —
surprised I'm not asked to stay!

'We're running an office here,'
he tells me, 'not a home' —
looking to his nodding team.

My report is official,
complete by noon. But I stay, all
day: they think I'll never go.

I won't. I'm waiting for the one
human error these P.O.
workers never counted on.

Uncle Rowley

One day on the bus he let
my brother have a cigarette.
I was about seven then
and completely out of it —
that Johnno who was ten
should be my uncle's friend.

I told my mother on them
and she rang Rowley next day:
his drunkenness in no way
was good excuse she said
to lead a ten-year-old astray.
And she cut my uncle dead.

The next morning he was round
and soon all were friends again:
I remember as he left
Rowley slipped me a smoke.
I could've been *ninety*-seven
I felt that much in heaven!

A House North Near Mangroves

You rarely see your face at
moments now that matter much.
It's when, say, shaving — and that's
once in a month at a stretch;
or tying a tie, adjusting
the noose for easy breathing.

How many, hearing the news
their grandfather died last night
in a house north near mangroves —
too far from where you are right
then at the moment you're told;
too late — how many have held
their face to a mirror that
moment? watched it in the wide
mirror above the driver's seat.

Instead of school as usual,
you are dressed up one morning,
bundled with fat sacks of mail
aboard a bus with your mother.
After you're sick of watching
cows watching each other,
you ask her *Where are we going?*
'Your grandfather. He died last
night.' And watch your mouth twist

to a great big question-mark.
You try twisting it further
over the driver's shoulder
till it makes you laugh. You ask
her again and keep watching
your face. *Mum where are we going?*

Song After the Search

The plain-clothed Johns
asked you yesterday
just what you were —
molester of young girls
writer of songs
stealer of pearls? —

and asked if they could
with no warrant search
your house for some jewels
from down the street
(well knowing no magistrate
would say they could)

and turned it upside
down and up again,
and satisfied
your name was Keats
ignored the fresh
blood on your sheets.

Picnic

Bring your Sunday hamper
down to the cemetery today
there's space for all the family here

the kids can all run off & play
while we cut your Sunday booze
fine enough to get a tan today

so warm today you tan
your winter body changes for
some other man

so if I seem to snooze
don't let it worry you
I'm changing too

& leave no empties when you go.

August Steam

The lake made no sense early on:
driving down a slipway straight
two truant kids in a big V8
parking in a rain storm
huddled in beside the lake.

It made no sense then early on:
it wasn't till much later
we understood things better
nothing could go wrong —
you said let's drive forever.

We could only return:
the sulphur city drenched
steaming after rain: so ditched
the faithful love machine
made in for a dressing shed.

Undressed each other in turn:
I never thought I'd ever
be your winter hot-pool lover
until I was right then.
Some things are never over.

A Wind of Wolves

The first page of *Zhivago*
the boy is on a mound of clay
beside his mother's grave.
My friend's funeral today,

already rain
at 5 a.m. An upstairs guest,
I hear a wind of wolves,
no flowers by request.

Collision

I took the punch like glass.
I didn't break, I shattered.
A car smash once, head on.

One day I started reading poems
where people said they looked out
crying through their tears —

I believe in all these things —
like looking at you dead
through shattered glass.

Bracken Country

Walk the wagon line
Embankments either side,
A half full flagon, harsh dry wine,
Underneath your arm.

The folks back home
Call you by your name.
Walk, son, drink, speak well of every
Single one of them.

After Sickness
(for Jerry)

Watching you paddling belly down
out on to the Tasman
I thought of an old duck
beating for the air

thought of the grey morning men
the men who come to kill you,

last mad duck of the season

Roadsong Paekakariki

1

A time when many break —
the blue heron stands more
alone than ever before.
I'm on the road again,
a small town public bar,
wondering where they all have gone;

read in tonight's paper
a head-on collision
a mile down Highway One:
the car, a Chevvy, ran
right underneath a ten-ton
truck at sixty miles an hour,

no names in the paper,
they still have no idea
who the victims were
or even their sex —
by our mid-twenties
a few have made headlines!

2

A time when many break —
the boys who joined the clubs
the universities
Jaycees and well-paid jobs;
traded in their old V8s
for wheels less expensive —

where do they live?
I can count one or two:
one old friend, she came through,
alone, fighting, alive;
a few men, too. The rest,
they're dead . . .

the blue heron's more
alone than ever before,
the gulls have all migrated
off to the graveyard;
the second-hand car dealer
buys me a beer.

Four Cobweb Poems

1
I've even named him now
this spider on the seaward window of my shack

I've watched him grow
watched him spin his first bright web

And then one day first thing
at six o'clock one early summer morning

I watched my spider catch
his first black fly

2
I feel for him
my spider on the window

Felt nothing for his victim
the fat black blowfly

My spider and I
we feel for each other

Nothing much can ever come between us
That's why I let him have the fly!

3
My spider often used to ask me why
I wrote him cobweb poetry

I told him
I really didn't know

If he wanted answers to questions like that
he'd better go

Spin himself a bigger brighter web
and leave my seaward window

4
And this is now the end
the end of cobweb poems

A girl came to my house last night
spinning faster than a cobwebbed fly she was

She didn't like my kind of home
that was what she said

Then she killed my spider dead
yes that was what she did ...

So this, friends, this is the last bright cobweb poem!

King Bodgie

1

I first got a head for heights
one morning the colour of magpies;
climbed the knotted rope I'd climbed before,
clung panting to the first thick branch
knowing now I'd still go higher yet.
My heartbeat rose like vomit.

Once up above the thick close lower limbs
a man was on his own. It took a full reach
just to reach the next branch up.
I concentrated hard, forgot looking back,
planning later descent. I sat on top
sixty-five feet up, a head for heights; gum and sweat.

2

Years afterward a high-rise
window cleaning job sees me through hard times:
sandshoe ledges twenty stories
high above the city streets. . . . Nothing new,
I don't look down for those same reasons now.
It is something else, this looking in,

looking in from outside through a woman's eyes:
it's make or break, love or die,
this morning full of magpies,
King Bodgie of the Birds this morning here. . . . .
And a woman asks her man what makes him
take such risks with her!

Mean-Eyed Pete

Don't like that way
you sniff round my feet
after where I been
wondering where I'm at

Took your woman out
took her out last night
dropped her back home late
just about dead beat

You got a mean-eyed
look about you Pete

I can't help it mate
she keeps calling round
calling at my flat
you know I can't help that

tells me she wants me
all the time on heat
says she's through with you
hasn't told you yet

Yeah you sure got that
mean-eyed look on Pete

You tell me to get
get right on out
leave your little sweetmeat
leave your little heartbeat

leaving nowhere Pete
I'm moving round inside
eight inches up inside her
I'm staying right on here

So keep that mean-eyed
look about you Pete

Portobello Sunset

I read the skyline right to left:
a humpback hill, harpoons; and moving
left and south, dark Otago
valleys and the razorbacks run with light;
a firebreak or two. They disappear nowhere,
somewhere west.

Because it is evening the sun sets there:
a skyline of burnt-off stumps, jet
black as distant cattle moving.
Like this, last evening, your letter
telling me your love burns on. Forever.
My love too. No firebreak stops it.

Lyn

These are the waking hours, the hours between
two a.m. in winter and the dawn. . . .
Shaken trembling from a dream:
someone screaming: like a baby new born.

The hours closest to death, tumbling in
a darkness darker than the womb or cave.
It is impossible to sleep again,
too many voices: tall Mark; Dave

who never made it in that fat old mother-
fucking Ford V8 past Waiwera: dead
drunk with one hand on the wheel; the other
down some sheila's pants. That's how he died.

Impossible to sleep, too many voices:
Mark is telling someone something: to do
with bikes for sure; his wild horses.
I listen now. You're next, Lyn. I wait for you

and sure enough, you scream!
You're dead. You may as well have not been born. . . .
I find my poems are written down between
two a.m. in winter and the dawn.

Modigliani Girl
(a faded denim blues)

You came one day
cute little dress
long brown neck
yeah you made me 'come
a nervous wreck

Yeah in you came
drove me mad
my mind aswirl
my mod Modigli-mod
li-ani Girl

Said you'd stay
then yesterday
you went away
left me with the faded
denim blues

Go on take my jeans
walk on down
the pathway home
your little Levi bum
zip still half undone

Denim blues
my mind aswirl
you drive me mad
my mod Modigli-mod
li-ani Girl

Just Like That!

So close, the poisonous berries
so close! Lying where you are
so close, this minute here,
you reach out and pick
a cluster of orange-red berries;
pop them in like jaffas. You
can be a child again, eat
more than's good for you —
here! like this — die
this minute here now where you lie.
One two three, that's it,
just like that!

Jim Died; Jerusalem Survived

Jim died; Jerusalem survived,
the kids in the house up the hill
'no more though than ten at a time'
Jim, their Hemi, lies outside

I went there today, up the mad
road, Koriniti (Corinth) up
Ranana (London), Maori kids at
every small town on a gate . . .

Like tired pop stars, sick of all the
big publicity, the ten
surviving commune members greet me,
talk proudly of their Hemi

I notice the wall telephone; seems
strangely out of place. 'Hemi, you know,
phone calls all the time!
It's been cut off now though'

Notes from a Journey
(*for Hone*)

When I left Wanganui
(you and Eve asleep still
low under canvas) my pilgrimage
was northward up
the river of the three taniwha

The sun shone; every little
township had its one-way bridge.
By midday, man, it seemed
a month instead of
half a day since leaving

Three o'clock that afternoon
I picked up three local boys,
Tawe, Gabriel, Andrew;
drove them through
Pipiriki out to Raetihi

They told me of Hemi, how
a month ago he walked
the whole way out on foot
'27 bloody miles of it!'
He died soon after that

'What if we meet old Hemi
around the next bend?' I asked.
'Let the bugger walk it'
one boy laughed. I turned
laughing with him

His face was dust and tears.
I passed him the bottle,
double declutching,
chopping down the gears.
It was a steep, slow climb.

We Could Just Disappear

We disappear,
ten carriages of us,
a tunnel as long as
tomorrow, next term,
a tunnel as long as next year,
as long as time.

No one knows when
we will come out the other end —
we could go on and on and
on forever and never
come out again.
We could just disappear.

When He Died

When he died a dozen men or more
Sold right up, packed up their little homes
Their families and all they called their own,
Moved inland well away from that cold shore.

That's how it is with such a man —
That when he dies he leaves men on their own
As if betrayed, as if without a home.
They're good friends though; all good men —

When visiting, they all agree how wise
He lived alone.... They watch the tide
Run in; now out; just like it always was.
But even this changed somehow when he died.

I Cried for This Man

It is never before I have cried at
The death of a man I never met —
Nothing at all to do with sentiment

I knew no one who knew him to set
Tears flowing with some whisky anecdote —
The sort of story you hear of the great

How he kept his old mother in comfort
Kept a great mansion for the down-and-out —
I knew no touching stories like that

The reason, pure and simple, was the thought
That when a man dies, then, man, that's it —
I cried for this man, quite by accident

Warm Ashes

I know to write you such a poem
when tribute verse is out of time
will make them puke. May it. It is
something between the two of us:
that when you died, warm ashes in
a wind near Albany, no one
there was sober; not enough to
remember where they threw you

Years afterwards your friends gather.
Your death holds them together.
One such time a few decided
to mark the spot. And so they laid
a stone in memory of where
most of them agreed they were.
Like the day they all got drunk,
your old Dally mate turned on the plonk

Leaving school I thought I would do
my bit and more: remember you:
packed a bag, a bottle or two,
went and lay beside that stone.
Later on I hitch-hiked on,
another town, another home,
the same old sleeping bag, one more poem.
Fairburn, all to do with you

I Kiss Your Hands

≪ *Baciamu li mani* ≫ *Questo, non altro.*
Oscuramente forte e la vita
                    Salvatore Quasimodo

Those big eyes, deeper, browner
now than ever before,
they don't pretend a thing,
ultimate recovery, anything like that.

A man who weighed ten stone
two months ago — now
not a half of that —
his eyes tell me all of it.

I try for soft words to console
the widow-to-be. They fail
naturally as our silence does.
Those eyes have said it.

I'm allowed no more than a minute.
Never have I tried to make
one minute last as long. His eyes look back.
They have already made it.

The Quiet Places

The truant schoolboy lakes,
inlets, estuaries,
still water;
every duck an apex
as it sailed away

We used to watch them
for hours as children;
sometimes we swam together.
My friend was the daughter
of a very old man

She never spoke of him,
her strange old man.
But when night time came
she always ran
the whole way home.

New Year '73
(Mr Rainbow Man)

Firing the garden hose
straight into the New Year sun,
water into sunlight,
I create a rainbow

and turning the nozzle from
narrow beam to wide fan,
the sun itself dripping,
I lengthen my rainbow

Each year, worse, this
arrogance. Creation bows.
I am God, I have
control of the rainbows

Con the Man/Melissa

His old man guts must rumble now,
In love with her not half his age:
Her weekend young men come, his scourge
Make love like he will never know

The only love in my life's been
A girl I met of seventeen
Melissa was her name

It's Monday through to Friday when
Men must work from nine to five,
It's then the old man comes alive
It's then he has her on her own

We could have always stayed as friends,
Kids sailing boats, had not our fronds
Of love been turned to shame

Monday through to Friday with
Weekend pleasure launches snoring
Nudging at their heavy moorings;
It's then the old man knows his worth

Twisted by a jealous few who fought
With stories that she felt I thought
She was just easy game

And many men like him are seen
Go through the Heads, the fishing fleet,
Heading for where the shelf is flat:
A fisherman, he had no son

We never met again and so
I had no chance to let her know
  I loved her just the same

This girl on land would easily be
Young enough to be his daughter though:
He brings his catch home to her through
The harbour heads, across the bar

To let her know I loved her for
Herself: she needed nothing more:
  But she, she never came

Four to five days every week,
It is like this, a lover's way —
Shacks on stilts right round the bay —
Loving and fishing is our work

So now I've turned into a rum
And brandy man, I'm sixty-one,
  Whom only death will tame

And there is a girl, I hope she knows
I sing of her, the new moon of her nose:
  Melissa is her name

Come Friday though, old Con the Man
Buries himself deep in last week's
News and drinks and dreams until he wakes.
The girl he loves loves younger men.

Storm, Bottle Creek

Late.... Nothing has been heard
of two local fishermen since Monday night.

To sea, salt wind; the rain is salt.
Nothing for three nights now; no word

save LIGHT, DARKNESS, names
you want to have in capitals and

shout to wake the world into the wind;
enough of storms.... .

Turn to the gaunt kitchen, load
logs that smell of salt on the fat stove,

smoke in bloodshot eyes: enough of
storms, mornings

the colour of lead;
fill hot-water bottles for bunks,

prepare for dreams;
the fishing-boats tugging at ancient moorings.

Daddy Dad on Fire

First it was a Sunday
Then it was a Monday
  Daddy used to come
  home every night

One night a lady came
Don't know why she came
  Daddy used to come
  home every night

I cried out my eyes
Wondering where I was
  Daddy used to come
  home every night

Dreaming of a mountain
I could hear my father shouting
  Daddy used to come
  home every night

Heard the front door slam
The last we saw of him
  Daddy used to come
  home every night

I've known many men since
One, some kind of prince
  Daddy used to come
  home every night

My man accuses me
Of infidelity
  Daddy used to come
  home every night

Puts on this jealous moan
About some other man
  Daddy used to come
  home every night

It's him I guess I'm waiting for
Drunken Daddy Dad on Fire
  Daddy used to come
  home every night

  Daddy used to come
  home every night

  Daddy used to come
  home . . . .

Early Opener

Why stay sober when
all the weatherman
predicts is rain

Belfast, Dublin, Cork . . . no big bomb scares here
up Molesworth Street, the Hotel Wellington,
   an early opener;
the last before a man clears clean out of town

A 15-stoner rises from his chair
already pissed and dancing like a queer:
   a day on full pay,
the wharves closed down for wet weather

A long-bar heater just above head height
burns your eyes until they smart,
   your forehead sweat,
makes your heartbeat rise like vomit

In walks the regular-most-regular,
bulldog 'Champ' with overshot jaw,
   alcohol and cold;
trembling with the early morning laughter

He sways, lurching under pats, between tables.
We talk all morning of the world and what it
   says in the paper.
'Champ' champs beer from a bowl marked 'Champ'

This morning's *Dominion*, the IRA
made headlines, man: among these latter-day
    New Zealand Irish,
any news is news, news from faraway

And any good moment now, old Brendan himself
breathing heavy from a heavy night before,
    Death himself warmed up!
His dreams were words. He clears the upper shelf

The Archangels themselves, I am told,
old Lucifer and all his irate union men,
    argued it out
in this very pub. They complained of the cold

These voices are voices in a sad dream,
faces of a last Irish sunset... 'Fed up,
    fucked and far from home';
defrocked bishops, every lone one of them

St Patrick's dead drunk in the Serpent Bar,
'Champ' is asleep, bloated on black 'n' tan:
    this early opener,
her doors wide open to all lost men

   Why stay sober when
   all the weatherman
   predicts is rain

Stabat Mater

My mother called my father 'Mr Hunt'
For the first few years of married life.
I learned this from a book she had inscribed:
'To dear Mr Hunt, from his loving wife.'

She was embarrassed when I asked her why
But later on explained how hard it had been
To call him any other name at first, when he —
Her father's elder — made her seem so small.

Now in a different way, still like a girl,
She calls my father every other sort of name;
And guiding him as he roams old age
Sometimes turns to me as if it were a game...

That once I stand up straight, I too must learn
To walk away and know there's no return.

Himatangi

When Leo died, his widow Mrs Sim
kept the corner wine-stop running; the roadside
macrocarpa hedge neatly trimmed as ever

W-I-N-E it is clipped to spell. Make time, stop there,
vineyard prices (cutting government tax).
She's housed men on the run since World War One

Inside the house, photographs in sepia:
Leo; Lenin; dead comrades round the walls;
play the player piano; plan the Revolution

A little lady giving the Red Guard sign
(the right fist raised), she showed me the moon,
'There's a hammer and a sickle up there too!'

Mrs Sim, because of you the moon
will always be a sickle; the hammer
raised, the ceaseless beating heart of a man

Four Bow-Wow Poems

1
You woke my mother up this morning
At six o'clock with your barking

So she took away your barks
And put them in the bow-wow box

She tied you up she took your barks away
Now all you do is smile at strangers all day

You aren't a guard dog anymore
You aren't even a dog anymore!

2
I don't really think I like
A dog that can't bark when he likes

So all by myself this afternoon
I took the bow-wow box down

It was hidden in behind a lot of books
And I gave you back eleven big barks

You've run outside to use them up
I think you've woken the baby up!

3

Look, here are some simple facts:
You'll find in the poetry books
One thousand and twelve poems about cats

There are all sorts of poems about cats:
Cats chasing rats and cats wearing hats
And cats that simply sit on mats

But you look for bow-wow poetry
And it's quite a different story
Right now there are only three

And one more makes four . . .

They often ask me why
I write this bow-wow poetry

I'll tell you
And cross-my-heart it's true

I've got nothing else to do

Sunday Morning Requests —
for the Children

And now we hear this story —
Robin Hood, Tom & Jerry —

Tom the Cat is chasing
Jerry through the forest

Out steps this big man 'Little John'
Shouting loudly SHAKE PAWS

And as I wake this morning
I am busy shaking yours

The Shallow Stream
through the City Floats

The shallow stream through the city floats
detergents, blood, waste from the valley
suburb up behind.... Late Friday nights
look beautiful, the children tell me,
the Town Centre, the big orange lights;
late shopping.

      A fortnight now I've been
a teacher up this State suburban
valley full of kids; do nothing else
than wander through the school, class to class,
'the poem man', showing the kids and teachers
games they can easily play with words.
Everyone shouts to make himself heard.
They soon find out how far from hard
it is to talk, to make up colour
poems, songs round sound; soon discover
the thing they shout about will never
be that exact same thing again.

            Strange —
their words give the stars a new hard edge;
streetlights or a flower, another tinge.

And every afternoon I hitch-hike out
the valley down to town; drink at
the fibrolite barn of a tavern....
Late shopping night tonight, I stayed on.

No more than ankle-deep, I later
waded down the stream. The bright lights were
floating on the late night stream through town;
the supermarket neons flashing
off and on and floating upside down.

Porirua

A Long Time

A long time now and everyone
let us know what they think best,
tells us what we should have done—
stay together, love; or bust.

We're given a final warning
today after a long time talking;
and in the mist of the morning
my love and I go walking.

The Windows of Our Morning

The mists descend again — no
plate-glass hillside view today

You wake in tears — no
recriminations now

> *that's all over*
> *be my love or*
> *show me the door*

I've said it all before — no
recriminations now

> *I love ya (yip!)*
> *w' all m' heart*
> *an' y' know it*

The mists a long time ago
surrounded us

The windows of our morning
burst into light; into tears

Your Ultimate Accountant

Your ultimate accountant:
You should have made him years back:
Someone should have told you that:

A man with muscles for cheeks,
Cheeks where his muscles should be:
New Zealand's Mussolini. . . .

I'm just a lover in black
Bloodshot from a bout of you:
I have long since turned my back

Long since known just what to do:
Beyond all proposition
I've joined your Opposition.

Caroline

The easy ladies all gone home,
moonlight, night for a poem,
a line that none of them
have ever heard: all to do
with the moon; for you.

The moon tonight in tears,
a bald bulb of light.
She has nothing to cry for.
She has never lost a child;
is never to have one.

Birds cannot fly by her.
Owls, you say, what about? Owls,
they fly by the stars, Pavo
north to the Pleiades: one by
one, they all fly home.

Cook Strait, Barranca. Moonlight
lays it like a riverflat,
easy as a breeze through poplars!
fishermen in thighboots drowned. She
knows nothing of that.

We cannot count dice by the moon.
Better we toss knucklebones,
small, bald, five white moons;
ignore her, utterly. Give her
something to cry for.

No Blue Moon

The moon keeps me warm—
And I, I'd never
never have ever
said that before—

I sweat under her—
She covers me like
a white feather quilt
the hottest nights.

My mother taught me
the moon was cold;
taught me the stars, taught
me all she could—

Praise her well tonight
and words in her praise:
ease up on her, her
fullness tonight—

The moon is not blue
(that's, least, some relief)
and she shines for you.
And that's belief.

A Blues Harp Blues

Auckland last December
telling poems and roadsongs,
forgot a line, kept my tune,
sang new words in time.

The song was one I'd one time
written you, to do with some
midwinter storm to some soft rhyme;
lost my song in front of them.

The next day south, hitch-hiked home,
found your note that read *I've gone
for good, goodbye!* . . . the same
sad tune; another song.

A Lonely Man (She Says)

Why yes, I saw him with his
Head bowed down, kicking a stone—
I thought, 'There goes a lonely man!'
Why, any such man I've known
There's always been good reason
Why he's always alone.

Not that I know him at all.
But any time we've met
He's always cornered me
With some intellectual argument—
Gary and I, you see, don't
Like people like that.

But you ask what is wrong
Kicking stones along the ground—
But you must do something in life!
I know he would say I sound
Like any Plimmerton housewife—
But all he does is muck around.

Worse than all this though,
He's such a damned show-off!
He seems to get some pleasure
Living that sort of life—
Wandering around all on his own—
I tell you, it's not good enough!

Before I forget though,
Tell me, is he on the phone?
We're having a party you see,
We would like him to come ...
(They say he can be such fun
If you catch him on his own).

Matins

Last night he made his final
heartsob and sorry call
this morning didn't even
wait the early mail

Threw the dog the phone book
skipped breakfast altogether
didn't even care to look
outside to check the weather

Sort of wondered if he should,
thought *fuck it mate why not,*
she's gone, this time for good!
opened wide and blew the lot

Buried Alive

I am scared of the dark,
I'm terrified,
I lose myself, I'm
swallowed up by it
as if I've died.

Worse than that, it is
as if I've been buried
and slowly now I'm
coming to, my mourners, my
mother gone home.

I feel for my body,
try recalling who I am,
feel for weight, dream
of things familiar
that bear my name.

Worse than any nightmare,
this dream comes true:
no darkness like it,
nothing I can do but
curl up without you.

Black Cattle at Dawn, Waiura

The fat black cattle
never seem to sleep

all night in the lower
paddock by the river,

like lover to lover
mooing to each other.

It's not as if they
do much else by day,

just watch one another
watching each other,

eyes wide brown and deep
don't earn a wink of sleep.

Part of the dark,
one-ton chunks of it,

the fat black cattle
awkward and bored

when first light spreads out
like the river in flood.

Call it the dawn, the Lord,
the Promised Land; whatever

what just a moment back
was a black black lake,

is now the lower paddock
in a full flood of light.

No transformation from Heaven
no light burst for them—

silhouettes left over
from the night before,

this moment of the Lord—
they are the one thing ignored.

Of the White-Faced Blue Heron

A feminist party,
Hamilton, jokes about
airline hostesses,
their regulation cunt
deodorant: 'Morning
Mist' it's called.

         I call these
women dancing smelly.
They play Helen Reddy,
hold hands, call each other
sister, sweetheart, mother.
Enough for a day!

         this
slow train south, back to
Bottle Creek where men are
men; evenings the hills
dissolve, the white-faced blue
heron fades: slow dreams: by
night, stares out the moon.

A Birthday Stone for Rebecca, 10

This stone is the egg of some
extinct bird. The bird is nameless;
its egg, solid marble. Take it to
your heart, warm it well. One day
you will give birth too.

Every Time It Rains Like This

Every time it rains like this:
rain from early morning falling
thick with light: the whole
wide world of our bay
has given in: rain: and nothing any
friend or fisherman can do

Every time it rains like this:
oilskins sweat in boatsheds:
well indoors: all's gone on for
far too long. . . . I am
one with rain, no longer to
that woman there; we're through

Every time it rains like this:
I walk hangover beaches, make
no more sense of it:
in love with a winter woman,
a woman when she steams, I kiss
wet winter lips, return to you

Every time it rains like this

Jacob and the Five-Pound Kelly

Hearing sad news of Jacob,
I took myself outside with
the five-pound Kelly; chopped
deep through the crust of the earth:

chopped like a madman, turned the
soil over, hacking it: then
fell back and slept, convinced
the earth would breathe again.

Until Day Breaks

His darkness it is utter, darker than
merely loss of light; midwinter sleep. . . .
His première! all sequences complete,
complete control for the rest of the night,
every image cut to fit;
nothing extraneous. He chews at his sheet.

He listens for his audience. Their shuffling
reminds him of the giant rosemary bush
against his bedroom window. It kept him
wide awake all childhood until he left home.
They smell vaguely, this audience,
of the aunts at his father's cremation.

Full house as usual, the midnight-
ramblers' special matinée! booked-out by
night-watchmen out of work; insomniacs. . . .
He never meets them. He knows them though,
knows what they like. He does his act,
keeps them quiet until day breaks.

A Minstrel Bow-Wow

Since this dog strayed into my life
I have been out hardly at all

Instead have started to move
In a totally new kind of circle

Within the four walls of this one-
Roomed boathouse-on-stilts called Home

I am a totally new kind of man
Bow-Wows and Bones less alone

Winter Dream

The wind blows cold still, easing up.
The cold tap's dripping melting ice.
The heat-pipe knocks: dead grandad and his
girl up there I guess

Skeletons upstairs! ... don't let up
you bastards you your lovely crimes,
we're in for thaw. We're in for
let's hope brighter times

Time to Ride
or *The Last Time I Saw Larry Happy*

The last time I saw Larry happy
He was driving a Ford V8 truck
Clapping down in top Moonshine Valley:
Thumbed him down, knew I was in luck.

Drove the drunk Horokiris, foot down flat,
A couple of tired old V8 louts
Going thin on top, fast going to fat,
Ten years of heavy drinking bouts.

Larry seemed changed, like he didn't belong,
Seemed like he had nowhere left to drive to:
Something had somewhere gone wrong:
Whatever it was, neither knew.

We drank out that day at the Paekak pub,
Got cornered by some smug suburban fool.
He kept baiting Larry, 'Won't you ever grow up?
You can't spend your life playing pool!'

Larry cracked later. I took it first,
Nothing much more than a mid-twenties menopause,
Nothing much more: never thought it would last;
Never a moment suspected the cause.

Time to ride ... I know in a way it was.
Larry's changed, has friends who are witty and
    waspy.
Larry's changed, will never be like he was
The last time I saw Larry happy.

Blackandblueblowflies

A talk-back show this morning
they talk of baby bashing.
Some mother from Brooklyn or Wainui
tells of bashing him black and blue.
She is in tears before the host
has time to cut her off.

             Another ghost
I had until today forgotten stirs,
blackandblueblowflies,
the path home from kindergarten.
Then I would tumble down the narrow
steps of the giddy jarra bridge and,
fast as my legs could go,
run home along the beach
where my mother slept in lupin.

No one it seemed had ever seen
blackandblueblowflies.
But that wasn't why the tears. . . .
There just never was enough
of any one mother or any
one around to cut me off.

Sugar Daddy Dirge

Dead Dad Dead
Hard life you had
Dad Dead Dad
What's in your Head
Worms Dad Worms
Worms for a brain
Prayers for the dead
Dead for the worms
Daddy Dad Dad
Rain Wind and Storm
Rain Daddy Rain

Christina 2

I dream these nights of webs
and black spiders swinging:

my last circus I saw a man
swing the width of the Big Top:

everyone clapped: he bowed he
wore white supports on his wrists.

The lions and the tigers: one
jumped through a high hoop of flame:

I thought of you; mistook
their clapping for rain on the roof:

silence: then on came
a dark dancing Russian:

she climbed the rope to the very
top of the tent. She danced

turning over: they found a bird,
so rare they thought it extinct,

dead in the madhouse rafters;
black spiders swinging. She bowed,

everyone clapped. I came back
home, dreamed dreams of you who

I had imagined dead; everyone
clapping for more. They couldn't have enough!

Tonight is a web, Christina, black
spiders spinning; rain on the roof.

You House the Moon

You have moved in upstairs.
I don't know what you do.
Except at night I know you
Sit up late. You watch the stars

About all I know of you.
Merciless as migraine
You pace out my brain.
Maybe you want my view!

Headaches all the more.
I have this dream a load
Of timber's dumped on the road
Right outside my door.

One by one, just your way,
You drag each plank upstairs.
I see nothing for tears.
You hammer away

You house the moon. You join the stars.
You have come to stay

Tomorrow, South, Love, Yes

The taupata at my door
plays host to visitors; nods
sagely to a passing breeze;
bows low, so low, announcing
entry to a heavy wind.

These winds have travelled many
miles of sea coast from the north.
At Bottle Creek they ease off,
often stay the night. I could
make comparisons I guess.

I won't. Instead to say how
good it is to see you, you
young thing, lady, passing through.
Tomorrow, south, love, yes. The
taupata is dancing too.

Maintrunk Country Roadsong

Driving south and travelling
not much over fifty,
I hit a possum.... 'Little
man,' I muttered chopping
down to second gear,
'I never meant you any harm.'

My friend with me, he himself
a man who loves such nights,
bright headlight nights, said
'Possums? just a bloody pest,
they're better dead!'
He's right of course.

So settling back, foot down hard,
Ohakune, Tangiwai—
as often blinded by
the single headlight of
a passing goods train as by
any passing car—

Let the Midnight Special shine
its ever-loving light on me:
they run a prison farm
somewhere round these parts;
men always on the run.
These men know such searchlight nights:

those wide shining
eyes of that young possum
full-beam back on mine,
watching me run over him . . .
'Little man,
I never meant you any harm.'

Your Dictator Dictates

Firstly then, I am sole
Dictating Dictator of
Nations of course, your world; of . . . .
Skip the introduction let's! let's.
Make this informal.

I love you although I am
Not going to say it. I am
Loath to state or insinuate
It could ever be permanent.
Enough to say I love you.

Get it straight, straight from the start,
And don't let me corner you,
Don't let me bore . . .
Your heart, your mother's heart,
Your beautiful young sister's heart . . .

So much more! as they say and
So little time. Nothing is
Permanent. Meantime I am
Emperor. I dictate poems
Accordingly. They become law.

Parihaka Dreamsong

His echo lasted so long
We were listening to his words
A long time after the man
Had gone down from the mountain.
All we knew of him was his song.

The child who was with me said
'His echo must never die!
I will stay up all life long
Until I have learnt his song.'
All we knew of him was he was dead.

The child, I remember her,
She used to ride a white horse. . . .
I cannot see the mountain,
I am blinded by a white sun. . . .
I swear to the gods I hear her.

Herons, Ma, Bright Spinnakers

The simple things — yachts with spinnakers
Bounce as bright as beachballs with a
Big wind chasing them across the bay:

The white-faced herons as the sun sets
Settle in the pine and macrocarpa tops,
Dark trees that are their home:

These simple things — to close two tired eyes,
To shut inside myself these images,
They belong to no one else —

I wake in ruins, herons and bright spinnakers
Collapsing, worn out around me now;
My mother, crying as she dies.

Full Dawn Ahead

Setting sail for some new dawn
I am still a long night off;
beaches breaking white with surf:
3 a.m. ... The night itself
has woken up; the coastal
weather bulletin: 'Little
change expected in the next
twelve hours. The mists persisting':
could have told them that myself!

You would turn, like in a dream.
I tell you, never again
will I attempt to explain.
No more of your questions, please.
I cleared town, simple as that;
set my course for a star,
wind dancing drunk in my sheets:
I am the man I've always
been; you, the woman you are.

One Highway One

Hitting north and every mile
another mile away
Every town I travel through
another town between us
The way it's going to stay
just the way it is

four hundred miles
four a.m.
wide awake
hitting for home

Hard to talk with a smile
tougher trying to cry with one
Hitting north now and the sun
hitting on the road ahead
That's like it is with the sun
a long time after you're dead

four hundred miles
four a.m.
forgotten now
just who I am

No one ever taught me how
a man should say goodbye
Left a bunch of flowers
cheapest stalks by far
Point is like, I love you like I
liked no love before

four hundred miles
four a.m.
forget me girl
or where I'm from

Let me down just once too much
last thing you should have done
Cried how sad and sorry, girl,
sorry, just a bit too late
Hitting north into the sun
left you swinging on your gate

wide awake
hitting for home
four hundred miles
four a.m.

Goodbye (More or Less)

Nothing is ever lost—
so if it could not last
longer than a week or two,
that's nothing other than
the way things go — sort of
dust to dust.

The blowflies gather fast—
you are a long way past
mouth-to-mouth or iron lung.
Last week I called you love.
Today you're nothing more
than part of my past.

Of Dan and the Peacock

Of all the constellations,
Pavo the Peacock
is visible tonight.
Pavo has the whole
night to himself.
He struts terribly.

In our tangle of
fishing boats and baches,
the only light
is Digger Dan's.
He mends his net.
His lamp burns late.

Tomorrow night Dan
sails beyond Mana,
the whole of
Cook Strait to himself.
He will drag the dark;
bring home a peacock.

A Sick-Bay Bow-Wow

The dog's back leg ripped open,
Some weekender's possum trap:

Ignoring rage, I bind up
Minstrel's leg the best I can . . .

Then this most moving scene:
All the dogs of Bottle Creek

Come visiting. They know he's sick;
Bring him bones though times are lean.

Burial of the Dead

I read tonight the Burial of the Dead.
Good reading as the moon lumbers seaward
Heavy as a Bristol Freighter;
                         watched
Men clear their spring city of corpses.
Before the thaw they said, before the thaw.
Mass graves were dug for the townspeople.
Farmers from the villages rode in
Defending churches, their women and children.
Their corpses were returned by rail.
I saw paddocks. Thaw was setting in.
The country people sang songs of a new dawn.
They buried their dead, all the time singing.
It was springtime. And there was a full moon.

Otakou, Otago Peninsula

They fly their flags across the water
To show they're home, the brightly-painted
Cribs across the Gut. Next weekend is
Easter. Every crib will fly a flag.

Or so I'm told by those who've lived here
Years. Like Laughing Les; the rest of them.
We don't fly flags, our side of the Gut.
No point says Les, we're home all the time.

Madam Tomcat

Its arrogance, complete affront.
We felt almost indebted.
We even named it. Madam Tomcat.
We came to live with it.

It came, has come, to live with us;
Come to haunt us, see us out.
I dream of giving it its final clout
Its final shove.

It barely stirs; your belly purrs.
I stroke it numbly, dream of
Final cure. You're well past that.
You are not past love.

Liz
(with your left hand crippled)

I know your dreams are dreams of
waking with the man you love:

whoever in those dreams that
good man be, you have his heart. . . .

I dreamt last night of you, Liz,
you, and every man had eyes

for some bird else: we were at
some bar. You sat like a cat,

queen of your corner, sizing
each bird up, hypnotising

every feathered one. They slowed
together. Then in a cloud

they rose across the garden,
the moon herself now hidden. . . .

Planets and a thousand stars
retreated. You flexed claws

slowly, your left claw crippling.
I woke appalled, applauding.

Up Battle Hill

Trees move because the wind
moves them. They rock asleep.
The wind does not let up.
This moment has no end.

Light on the river moves
as if to move away.
Trees, wind, light, river, stay.
As you do too, far loves.

Peeping-Tom-A-Cold

I pass the house you're to move into,
Chop down a gear, chug slowly by.
Today with nothing left to do
I parked outside, a private eye!

Or peeping-Tom, I parked the truck
Where lovers still to come will come.
Coldly happy there, I took a suck,
Whisky bottle for a thumb;

Meant to stay all day. But fear,
A feeling some strange way, bereft,
Drove me away....I know I'll never
Visit you. I had already left.

Friend to Many
(in memory, Rupert Taylor)

The river runs through jonquils
Flowers on all the window-sills:

We will join you when we die
We will wander these green hills:

Friend to many, man, goodbye.

River Woman Songs
(for Kristin)

1
We have not made love
since I had to leave north

since our silver turned over
when the full moon was new.

We will make love tomorrow
every bend of the river.

2
I lie down with the lamb.
Survival is my game.

My dreams are of you,
of nights, days left behind;

dreams of slow daybreaks,
sun on iced paddocks.

3
A joyless journey north
a woman's twisted mouth;

she smiled at times when time
was running to her rhyme.

I knew I had to leave her,
join you by the river.

4

You wait first movements,
the kid inside you kicking.

I watch your eyes for hints,
each dawn, their flickering.

We walk by the river often;
a daughter or a son.

Two Winter Settings

1
I knew a girl who
came from where the blue
lupin flower grew, oh
such a girl I knew

where lupin flowers grow
as blue as her blue
eyes against the snow.
So, the girl I know.

2
Taiaroa Heads, I've never
seen them floating so, so
easy on the light as
land can float on sea.

Low cloud slides south;
the albatross lift off;
warm breezes blow. Far as
eye can see, and further, snow.

Ana Gathering Cones on Battle Hill

When I do not know of what
to sing or speak—what tune,
what word—I watch and wait
the slow rising of the moon:

the moon so slowly rising,
a man can only wait
and watch and maybe sing
songs, speak words, of love or hate.

The moon last night in storm.
I watched it rage above
Battle Hill until the dawn.
That song was one of love.

Up there today among those
pines, we could, you thought, have been
aboard some ship in wild seas,
creaking jib, rib and beam.

I know of the many moons,
the shadows and the phases.
I know of as many women,
sung them silver phrases:

a moon for the river,
another for the sea.
This moon, tangled as ever.
You, of these dark trees to me.

Girl with Black Eye in
Grocer's Shop

No hiding it, a proper
bloody mess. Lucky she's still
a left eye left at all.
She smiles back as usual.

The man she lives with — plans to
marry soon as his divorce is through—
he beats her up often.
Never quite this bad though.

About as much as we know.
No idea why: suspects some
other man maybe. No
difference, result's the same.

We know her scene by heart,
black eye, the bruises. Apart
from that, not a bad looker,
the sort of mystic hooker.

She smiles again, shows she's brave;
buys groceries for two, still in love.

Words on a First Waking

Recall those dreams — at 2 a.m.
you call them poems — that one of home,
your father, huge, alive; the rooms
of that old house, themselves like dreams:

you spoke of him, your dad, his forced
retirement. Clenched like a fist,
death by slow cancer. You went down
south to see him; found half the man.

Recall him now; recall that dream
you called a poem at 2 a.m.—
that world of house and father deep
down south. And so, you drift from sleep;

you dress. Deliberate; beautiful,
as if you had a wardrobe full—
the same tight jeans and shirt you threw on
yesterday. To think us strangers then:

all lovers like to think they're not!
It's your world, love. You wander out
alone into the living room,
alone into another dream.

Cuckold Song

We are not allowed to
Your old man's told you—
Don't ever trust that guy,
The one with freckled knees
A stutter and a sly
Old dog called Blue Vein Cheese.

But here we are together
Caught in carnal weather
Without a coat without
In fact a bloody stitch
Ready for another bout
Your marriage in the ditch.

Your husband was a cuckold
First time I saw your face
Days before we ever rolled
That man took second place.

Those prayers you know by heart—
Get down on bended knee
Pray he finds it in his heart
Forgive you girl for loving me.

Get back to your marriage
Back to your tidy man,
Forget your grief, your rage,
Who you are, who I am.

Those Eyes; Such Mist

Sea mists from the upper inlet
lift, the morning hills afloat.

I dream of the several men who've
sailed seven seas; their many mists;

wake again to your love
as thick dreams clear; a dream of masts,

a dream that no man ever
saw your eyes like this.

I have lost all voice. I kiss
those eyes, our voyaging; such mist.

No Exit
(for Michael Smither)

        box-thorn and bamboo
wind-breaks round the coastal farms:
narrow roads that only go
headlong for the sunset.

Bring tokens with you, charms;
a letter, stone or wind-chimes:
dreams from the world left behind
worlds behind the mountain....

Egmont dropping in the rear-
vision mirror as you drive
drunk with all love lost in mind.

You will know it somewhere near,
of this alone, quite certain:
a man can go no further.

Four Songs

1 Snow Song

'I miss you when it snows'...

But cynics say it snows
in that demented fellow's
country barely once a year...

I say (and pray you hear)

'it snows here every day.'

2 Love Song

I will hide in these dark trees.
  No one will ever
  find me here. An
animal, no more a man,
  crouched on hands and knees.

  So strange, my lover
lit in that great house below.
  She glows so; knows so!

  I will call on her,
make love to her, tomorrow.
  The taut bellied moon
  so low now, low. Soon
the sun must rise; I must go.

3 Boy's Song

Above our house there is a track.
It winds its way across the hills.
Hot afternoons the hills turn blue
And darker blue until they're black.

My father used to carry me
In a battered blue back-pack.
He used to take me high, high up
That winding high-hill track.

When I grew old enough to walk,
We walked together, my dad and me.
When I got tired he gave me piggybacks.
I sometimes fell asleep like that.

Last week I watched my father walk
Away from me, up that same track.
The hills have turned from blue to black
So many times. Still he's not come back.

4 Recitative: Cloudy Bay

White gulls blow inland now, your
eyes a winter closed. To say
we miss you's true. That we do;
wintered these months in the bay;

looking. No, not for you. We
know you're dead. Even the young,
those who don't remember you,
know that. Like they know your song:

they sing it every time they
see seagulls blown inland from
this winter shore. And true, they
sing that the drowned may hear them.

Wagoning, up Moonshine
(*for Kristin*)

He plucks cress; water runs muddy.
He bends to drink, his image blurs.
The stream runs clear. He drinks
Till short of breath, falls back asleep:

Dreams of hawks on the upper
Current of the Moonshine wind, of
This wind's low moan. His dream
Burns clear, of her; of making love,
Whisky from water so pure.

Assumption, 1975

Night Psalm

Night, (the black spider's web and the spider)
Melts. The hands of the morning are clean,
What he imagines are the hands of an angel,
Clasped and very white; very bland.... .

The light is folded so. So, the child,
Exhausted by warfare and demons, wakes.
Night, (the black spider's web and the spider)
Was better than this, this cloud, this white
    floating land.

My Father Today

They buried him today
up Schnapper Rock Road,
my father in cold clay.

A heavy south wind towed
the drape of light away.
Friends, men met on the road,

stood round in that dumb way
men stand when lost for words.
There was nothing to say.

I heard the bitchy chords
of magpies in an old-man
pine... '*My* old man, he's worlds

away—call it Heaven—
no men so elegantly
dressed. His last afternoon,

staring out to sea,
he nods off in his chair.
He wonders what the

yelling's all about up there.
They just about explode!
And now, these magpies here

up Schnapper Rock Road....'
They buried him in clay.
He was a heavy load,

my dead father today.

Blue Smoke Rings

I was hugging my father:
His chin bristly, the smell of his pipe
Strong as I ever remember.
I never smelt him so ripe:

I never felt him so; knew
Him two months dead; Christmas
My first without him. He blew
Blue smoke, blew me ripe kisses.

And I kept holding my father
Alive in my arms; knew then
He'd never die. When my father
Blew me blue smoke rings from Heaven.

Birth of a Son

My father died nine months before
My first son, Tom, was born:
Those nine months when my woman bore
Our child in her womb, my dad
Kept me awake until the dawn.
He did not like it dead.

Those dreams of him, his crying
'Please let me out love, let me go!'
And then again, of his dying. . . .

I am a man who lives each breath
Until the next: not much I know
Of life or death; life-after-death:

Except to say, that when this son
Was born into my arms, his weight
Was my old man's, a bloody ton:

A moment there — it could not stay —
I held them both. Then, worth the wait,
Content long last, my father moved away.

Drunkard's Garden
(*in tribute, Darkie*)

Like Old Man Adam did.
Or Darkie when he died.
Like any man who moves
to other parts, we leave
our gardens after us.

Others move in to them.
They tend them; call them home.
I've left behind my share
of gardens. Like lovers.
And I move into yours.

This overgrown acre,
full of empties, Darkie!
A headland, refuge for
the heron, swan and wild
duck and drunkard; lover, child.

Baptism by River Water

We have come a long way,
some would say too far;
beyond what others think
we should have done. You blink.
That was yesterday.

Your old man rose and spoke
of horses and love,
then turned into a tree;
which left just you and me.
I lit up a smoke.

Again, quick as a wink
and change of a verse,
today is tomorrow
and that is long ago.
Have yourself a drink,

watch the river below
make love with the light.
Together in this land,
much we don't understand.
Call it tomorrow.

The ancient clydesdale stands
still as the morning.
The trees now all that move,
a sigh of pines; rough love;
our laying on of hands.

The Grown-Ups

He points his torch at the moon:
Was told never to do
Anything naughty as that,
Anything so arrogant.
The moon, my boy, is important.
So he was told.

He knows all that to be true,
(To rhyme with told) now he's old.
But he still loves to point
His torch full beam on the moon;
Still does not know what they mean.
They say, 'A strange, silly man.'

Death of the Young Poet

He wrote of his verses in his journal,
'Popping up, their own sure, sweet way'

Not knowing then — nor does he know today —
The rhythms of the heart are never sure;

Sweet words will all one day be gall.

He wrote of those verses in his journal,
'I will live through these lines forever'

Believing in love — believing his lover —
that Man, and all that Man holds dear,

Will never die. 'And I will never fall.'

A Mirror-Kiss Goodbye

He'd sling his long slack
songs of love or lack
of love to sheilas,
easy lays:

his women all grew
older: he withdrew.
I dug a hole then
threw him in . . .

then as his last guest
I carried out his
last request:

sang as he always
liked it, oh, friend Those
Were the Days.

To Suffer You

Your demands sound simple. You
ask I suffer as women do;
suffer as only you can do.

To wake clear-eyed! Always
we must wake together, eyes
red, exhaustion and tears.

Your demands, quite simple.
They beat a man to a cripple,
make the proudest man humble.

And I oblige, do as you ask.
It is — and I quote — 'a simple task'
to suffer you.

For Kristin and Tom on a Stormy Morning

Last night the moon took one
Hell of a hiding: and then
this morning on the headland,
a colony of pied stilt, so
delicate, so very
timid really, in the
face of such a storm:
in military formation, they
stood it out and no
one budged or threatened them —
strength in numbers or some
such joke, I don't know! —

What I do know though,
that when I clambered up home,
my lady and baby both
brought back to mind that
battered moon, those small
brave birds in storm: so
timid at the window,
delicate and warm.

The Men of Moonshine
(in memory, Chris Glennie senior)

The men of Moonshine now
are not the men that were:
where Glennie fought the law
these play a weekend war.

Chris Glennie died a score
of years ago and more.

Another breed of man —
if breed of man he be —
has pitched his pre-built house
on hills for all to see.

One of such a lucky few —
an exclusive way of life —
he wouldn't swap his view;
would rather swap the wife.

Chris Glennie lived a score
of this man's days and more.

The mists beyond Rock Hinge —
the hills behind slam-to —
drink up, a one last binge,
last distiller of the dew!

The man in his new home
has ended up alone;
has ended having nightmares
he is not anymore.

Chris Glennie's come to haunt him,
to even up the score.

Dayroom Dreams

After many months' rain,
Allowed out to play again.
The puddles on the playground were squashed
    pumpkins,
Colour and shape. When no one was looking
I tried one for taste.
I picked it up and rolled it,
A hoop of watery sky, blotchy and humid,
Until it melted away.

There was an aim to the game
And a name attached to it too.
As captain, I dared not ask either.
Half-time they brought on
Warm orange juice in paper cups
I knew to be flat beer.

I woke with a craving for something chilled,
Stumbled punch-drunk to the fridge.
'Mother take me home!' She purred
Careful as a young politician,
Shelves stacked high with iced pints of blood.
I drank my first love's.

Some stay awake all night
Telling each other jokes
Or telling their listeners they never
Wished to get involved in the first place.
Others sleep — the dayroom is full of them —
Dreaming their dreams, half-time nightmares of home.

After the Hunt

Of these things I wonder —
the rise to the gallop,
the rise of blood; of her —
the hunted or the hunter.

I don't know which I am,
pursuer or pursued;
or which way to run, in-
side myself: or side

with them — walk out unarmed
and leave myself unharmed;
and leave myself, no more
myself; drink champagne,

make chat with her husband
on velvet lawns, share jokes —
nudge and a wink — make them think
I'm not a bad bloke.

But I'm no good at smalltalk —
the trapped fox in me screams —
so it's bad on the stalk,
it's back to bad dreams:

the wanted man, the man
who wants. I move in on my prey.
And blood everywhere,
to her I make prayer.

A Summertime Blues for Tom

The garden's gone to seed,
the grass is spiked with thorn.
My child has learned to walk
but cannot cross the lawn.

The sun strums louder now.
I tell him 'Tom, a young
boy's and his old man's blues,
they are the same when sung.'

He stumbles and falls, hot
tears down his cheeks. I try
to comfort him, but what
the Hell! we're born to die.

Salt Man
(for Frank Sargeson)

Some man called you once
Salt Man. I would not,
could not, better that.
Nothing's won by chance —
I know that now —
it's where you strike
that matters most. Like
nothing's ever new.

This, to do with you?
For sure it is, Salt
Man, your great heart's vault;
with all things true —
back-roads of the heart;
pub; the bull's-eye dart.

Sailor's Morning

Red sky at night
Shepherd's delight
Red sky at morning
Shepherd's warning

Storm light, red as the old shepherd's warning.
We always as children said 'Sailor' instead.
And always as children we were safe beside
A calm summer sea, blue in the morning.

I came down today like an outlaw to town.
The small local school was ringing its bell
Calling the kids from home, hot porridge, all
Those mornings ago I've nearly forgotten.

I make the gates, 9 a.m. I'm dead on time.
A newly-installed schoolmaster-cum-minister
Eyes me as if I were a child-molester,
Satan-returned. I'm just trying to get back home!

Imagine addressing the locals . . .
'Ladies and Gentlemen of my home town,
I returned this morning saddle-sore down
The valleys till I came to those skyline hills'

(I point out the window of the hall)
'Like every poor bastard born these parts
I cleared out soon as I could' (applause;
        paper darts)
'Now, Ladies, Gentlemen, I return to Hell:

I must inform you though, there's a price
   on my head' . . .
It is here I always come-to, shouting that
   warning.
And the light wakes me up, turning red,
Storm light, red as the old shepherd's
   morning.

We always as children said 'Sailor' instead.

Twelve Moon Lines

The complications of the night!
A moth caught up in a cobweb,
The moon caught up in cloud:

The night, so very difficult,
No wonder no one sleeps:
So difficult: and no one's fault

Except, of course, the moon's.
She has nowhere to land.
She has nothing to lend.

Her light is borrowed light.
The sun gives all; and rises soon.
The moth is tangled with the moon.

Return to Drunken Bay

I thought once if I one day
ever gave the booze away,

images would come my way
I never knew existed.

Instead I feel half-past-dead.
Friends they call me half-mast Fred.

Nineteen days and dry nights now
see me beached, a stranded scow

where white gulls nest, squawk and row:
nineteen nights and days now dry,

level-headed asking, why
stave off death, why even try?

I lie dead; like it somehow.
Gulls have taken over now.

All you have is this beached scow.
Listen, if you dare, for screams —

even the dead have their dreams.
Listen too for creaking beams.

Check for dry-rot; check each scar.
I let it all go far too far:

but like it, the way things are —
white waves near; one cold white star.

Return to Rangitoto

His days were full of maps
of places visited:
his nights as full of dreams
of friends long dead.

He had one tattered map,
island of black granite;
and one recurring dream
as sure as night.

All day on whisky he
would fight the demon drunk,
the nightmare-man who shared
his coffin bunk.

Two visions would not fade:
that map; that dream of her.
Most men pronounced him mad.
He did not hear.

He burnt that map — he had
directions well by heart —
he hit the road until
that road ran out.

The island was afloat,
volcanic on the light.
He was, men said, adrift.
I say, bereft.

Song for Tom

My son has come so far
to ask me something: what
I do not rightly know —
how far away a star?
how true, that stars burn hot?
how it is they glow?

I tell him, child, look,
these questions that you ask
have answers no man knows —
man writes many a book
just like he wears a mask.
Yet still the night sky flows.

He turns and goes away
outside into the dark.
I join him, take his arm.
There's so much left to say . . . .
Far, far off, farm dogs bark;
fall silent now. Dead calm.

Some Songs for a Hostess, Air New Zealand

Lady from Liverpool I know
so little of you now, so
lovely that you are I go
right overboard, can't
tell right no more from wrong;
just happy lady to
tell you how I like you,
fly with you; sing you a song.

Lady from Liverpool
you make me feel like I'm
a small kid back in school
waiting story-time:
I hear one tell of the lion,
of how he lay with the lamb.
An end to all crying.
That's lady like I am.

Winter here and it's cool,
a long way lady from
McGough, your Liverpool,
a long way from your home:
we are miles apart,
maybe where we should remain.
I think not, lady —
I must fly with you again.

A Bow-Wow Bay at the Moon

My life is a dog's life
And the dog's life mine!

Leashed to a thick dull chain
And told I have free rein

Fed like a phased dull wife
And kicked if I whine

A dog's life mine, the moon
And bones, both on the wane.

Another Bow-Wow of a Bay

My master reads his Yeats:
'A Great Dane who could not

Bay the moon; and now lies
Sunk in sleep.' I close my eyes;

My master sighs Shit Hot!
I fall asleep. I don't know

Yeats. Great Danes turn me off.
I dream of bones, barking as I go.

Rainbows and a Promise of Snow
(*for Alistair Campbell*)

1

Winter means one side or other of
the shortest day. Our birthdays both
are on that good side, friend, of
solstice. Winter is a warm hearth;

rainbows and a promise of snow.
Or so life's been for me this last
half-life of sixteen years. Days go
so very slow they say, so fast.

It matters not. A good mate dies,
another goes abroad or mad.
It matters neither way. What does,
what always will, is that we load

the fire high with logs. She's a
winter this! bull-seals barking in the bay.
If she don't snow soon, I tell you
friend, she's never going to.

2

Sixteen and just left school
I dumped my books and hiked
four hundred miles south;
hitched-up where I liked:

barbaric coast, barbaric winds
madder than I knew could blow:
what better making of friends,
a promise of snow.

I go to the river, friend,
walk along with the flow;
far as third bend,
far as I go:

remembering time goes
so very fast, so slow:
solstice and birthdays,
a promise of snow.

A mad wind has risen,
the bull-seals bark at the moon:
I have a knee-high son;
you, a grandchild soon.

My chance to wish you cheers,
we've many good miles to go.
Here's rainbows (whisky tears),
a promise of snow.

Call from Deaths Corner

Our phone line to the world outside —
this one of headland, ancient house —
a frail link! It disappears through ngaios
massive as the house. Where it goes
beyond those trees, I've never looked.

I find a number in the book
and dial it. They say they're licked,
their world at war. So, so distant,
hardly worth the keeping in touch —
but I do. And that's about it.

Death's Dance

Grandma Weldon at the local store
remembers well — a girl of four —

a party here: so many guests
that when they all joined hands to dance
they circled out the main front door
around the big veranda once,
into the living room then out
and down again the corridor —

'Remember that without a doubt!'
says Grandma Weldon at the store.

Words for the Poetry Teacher

Why ever teach a line
the child has to learn
by heart, before his time?

Better to let it burn.

Better to sit dead still
on sofa, bench or stool,
arms folded, back in school.

Know not a syllable.

Just like that sky-high pine
that sighs; that knows of pain;
that knows no need of rhyme.

So the child. So the rain.

Big Jim
(I.M.)

He took, he seldom gave;
was a poet and surfer.
As both he always
missed the lyric wave —

so when it suited him
was want to tell lies,
Big Jim. Strangely, the
women liked his eyes.

West Coast Woman

I thought I had arrived; that this —
the shaking of hands, kisses from
strange ladies, speeches from a mayor —
I took this as arrival;

accordingly unpacked my bag, took a
stroll around the town, took a
show in with a stranger, later
stoned, made love with her.

Was I to be blamed? I was,
and for that matter, am, the
sort of man that people
point out as a man who has,

despite himself and those
who spite him most, arrived.
I felt so utterly
sure, surrounded as I

was by trappings such as these
I took for real; was had:
but come to understand it now,
understand your absence, your

refusal to join such mad
back-stabbing crowds: come
now humbled, to the closed
door you open.

Death of the Poet Preacherman

His tendency to preach through his verses
Became in the end, the critics agree,
His end. Abandoned by his images
Of stars and apple trees in bloom, the sea,

Of mountains melting to the sea, he died.
His funeral was packed. The critics and preachers
Made speeches, cracked quips; a few even cried —
Their universities and churches

Closed for the day. The only place open —
And where he would have been himself had he
Not been waylaid, packed in a box to ripen —
The Peep-O-Day. They drank the house whisky,

Recounted anecdotes: and all of them
About his drinking bouts; none to do
With blackouts, starless nights, spring without bloom,
Hangover mornings forever without dew;

Those he loved and lost. Or how, when he lost,
Refusing sentiment, he took up, rather,
Role of preacherman-in-verse; sort of priest,
Confessor, drunkard; sort of, my father.

Of the Star of Dead Cold South

The light is white, topside of the leaves.
Their underside is dark, reflecting earth.
Such honesty! unknown of the mirror.
We see in mirrors what we want to see;

and so with telescopes. I watched for hours once
a star astronomers all said was dead.
I wrote a poem about its so-called death —
a song of birth — Star of Dead Cold South.

I felt I was the shepherd, king or prince,
witness of this miraculous birth. . . .
Sunrise, the sun rose! blotted out the night.
My star faded; poem turned dark; to the earth.

Man Walking Home Late, Contemplates the Bow of Wow

Or is it worth it, so
You ask? Just watch him go —

No barking now — a ghost,
Marking every lamppost,

Checking out the night, for stiffs,
For cops, for busts at dawn . . . .

A dark night this, he sniffs
The air, suspecting storm.

Games of Patience

I never was a man for playing cards,
could never hope to keep a poker face;
was never part of any school. The pace
just was not mine. I went more for the bards;

ignored the others gathered in a ring.
Some kids had Playboy packs, a naked
woman every suite or every card.
I liked to dream more of the real thing.

I miss them though, those kids, now men; would back
them any day if I'd the gambling skill.
Now overseas, they keep the same old school.
I come to shuffle, deal, a private pack:

at airports, quayside pubs, the farewell shouts,
promises to keep in touch; photographs
for wallet-keepsakes . . . . I get my laughs
reshuffling them today, their passport shots.

April Fool

It's the old tricks is best tricks
cause only the best tricks survive

So,
up behind our hill
behind the macrocarpa belt
this God-almighty glow.

A fire first I thought how will
the engine ever get up there?

I changed my mind I thought those
new neighbours they're
always having parties.
Not like at our place.

I clambered up, wanting most I guess
a rock-and-roll band whacking
shit from up the hill. Floodlights,
everything I thought the whole
damn lot.

Instead, full on and lifting
out of heavy cloud,
the moon. Up to her old
tricks I thought.

Four Manly Verses

1

So much bare flesh, so very
smooth, brown as any berry,
utterly untouchable,
a man can only babble,
dream the unattainable,
stutter the impossible.

2

The loneliness of summer,
the over-forty runner:
SWIM BETWEEN FLAGS!
RESCUE PHONE ONE-ONE-ONE:
once a man has blown
youth, oh, once the bird has flown,
man drowns alone, blood and bone.

3

The fat and middle-aged all
out in force, out for a ball:
all end up in the kitsch
lounge bar perving at the beach;
sun, salt; the seven-year itch;
the gold flesh out of reach.

4

Meantime, lover by lover
the young in the sun, never
heard of cancer of the skin;
horizoned there, the dorsal fin;
ever asked the price of sin,
Sonya, Barry, Brian, Lyn.

One Way Bridge

1
The words just written
to give you warning

I'm not here to be bitten

did not exist this morning;
would have had no meaning.

2
So sad, the song sung
for you, dull spinster

composed for this occasion —

I won't be here this winter
nor the next one either.

3
Almost evening now,
little left of day,

little left to say that's new.

The sign-posts insist, ONE WAY
BRIDGE. Sorry, I cannot stay.

The Last Time I Saw Larry

He always slept in the living room,
his mattress on the floor in the corner.
He liked to be part of the action,
to be part of any conversation

awake or asleep. He was always like that:
liked to know nothing in the house took place
without his (no matter how passive) involvement.
Life, awake or asleep, was for Larry a race.

So little wonder then, to me and his mates,
that when Larry was hit by leukaemia
he'd have nothing to do with hospitals —
said he'd rather give medicine his balls!

and used to quote some bit of Oscar Wilde
to do with not minding what people said
behind his back — so long as he heard them! —
his wide eyes tired, his laughter mild.

I was back at the house today. Larry's bed —
and to see it made your heart feel like lead —
there in the corner. And Larry there, listening.
We miss you old mate, we're sorry you're dead.

Requiem

They say 'the lighthouse-keeper's world is round' —
The only lighthouse keeper that I know
Inhabits space, his feet well clear of ground.
I say he is of light, of midnight snow.

That other lighthouse keeper — he they say
Whose world is round — is held responsible
For manning his one light by night; by day,
For polishing his lenses, bulb and bell.

My man, my friend who lately leaves, is quite
Another type. He climbs no spiral stairs:
But go he does, for good, to man the night;
To reappear, among his polished stars.

Hilary

(for Hone Tuwhare)

I too had a lean
Aunt. She died at thirty.
Like yours, from Tb.
She was a cross between
mother and sister
but better than either.
She left five kids, and me.
I was aged ten
in the middle of winter.

A northern cousin
found a bird dying that morning.
He brought it to his mother, Joan,
one of Hilary's three sisters.
Joan froze. Then burst into tears.
She knew it was Hilary,
the youngest and most frail,

the one who wrote poems,
the one they called
'the Little Poet of Pangatotara',
the one who never got over
the flood of '54,
the year the Motueka River
rose and covered the farm.

There was silt through everything.
There was silt through Hilary's lungs.
She had strange dreams
the whole of that last year.

One, about me —
I have her letter still
telling of how
I'd one day walk out on stage.
Who would have believed it!

Hilary did.
And not long after, died.

I went by the farm today
but didn't go in.
Her husband lives there still,
a prosperous farmer
who dabbles in the arts,
happily remarried.

I could only watch
the river flow past the farm,
the Tasman mountains heave through mist,
the poplars hold the light apart.
And I thought for
a moment I saw
Hilary wave from the farmhouse door.

The rain quickened.
Soon everything —
the riverflat farm,
the mountains, river and poplars —
was blurred.

It was
years since I'd cried.

A Birthday Bow-Wow Blues

As a man grows older
His dog grows sadder

Not às many bow-wows, boy,
Not as many bones. . . .

If you're feeling old
This man he's feeling sad

His happy tales told,
His best times had.